SEP - - 2010

THE SKY TREE

THE SKY TREE

A trilogy of fables

by

P. K. Page

Illustrated by Kristi Bridgeman

OOLICHAN BOOKS

LANTZVILLE, BRITISH COLUMBIA, CANADA

2009

Library and Archives Canada Cataloguing in Publication

Page, P. K. (Patricia Kathleen), 1916-
The sky tree / by P.K. Page ; illustrated by
Kristi Bridgeman.

ISBN 978-0-88982-258-0

1. Children's stories, Canadian (English).
2. Fables, Canadian (English).
I. Bridgeman, Kristi, 1961- II. Title.

PS8531.A34S59 2009   jC813'.54   C2009-904759-4

We gratefully acknowledge the financial support of the Canada Council for the Arts, the British Columbia Arts Council through the BC Ministry of Tourism, Culture, and the Arts, and the Government of Canada through the Book Publishing Industry Development Program, for our publishing activities.

Published by
Oolichan Books
P.O. Box 10, Lantzville
British Columbia, Canada
V0R 2H0

Printed in Hong Kong

TABLE OF CONTENTS

A FLASK OF SEA WATER

1

Once upon a time in the mountainous, land-locked Kingdom of Ure, there lived a goatherd. And every morning when the dew lay in the valley, he drove his goats up to the high meadows where the air was clear and the grass was sweet. And every evening when the sun dropped behind the topmost peaks of the westerly mountains, he drove them down to the valley again. And the months passed, and the years, as peaceful and happy as the goatherd himself.

Now one day, as he and his goats were crossing the King's Highway, the Princess happened to be approaching in her carriage.

"Make way! Make way for the Princess!" cried her outriders, so the goatherd, herding his flock to the side of the road, stood respectfully back.

The Princess, who had been sleeping, was awakened by the noise and, curious, pulled aside her curtains just in time to gaze straight into the eyes of the goatherd. Never had the Princess imagined such eyes. Were they brown or were they gold? She could hardly tell. But they were more beautiful than any she had ever seen and they looked right into her heart.

And never had the goatherd imagined such beauty. A newborn doe, a pearly sunrise in the mountains, wild flowers in the meadow—these were all beautiful things, and each time he saw them his heart turned over. But the Princess was more beautiful still. Her hair was black and glossy as a raven's feathers and her eyes—how could he have known that eyes could be so large and so blue? Although he had seen her for no more than a passing second, he stood dazed, rooted to the spot, staring after her carriage until it was out of sight.

From that moment the goatherd's life changed. The face of the Princess filled his dreams; it accompanied him on his walks to the high pastures. Where once he had seen flowers and the first small strawberries, now he saw only the Princess. Waking or sleeping he could think only of her.

Finally—unable to bear his life without her, and determined to see her one more time—he left his goats in the care of a trusted friend, slung his goatskin over his shoulder and set out on the long, hard road to the palace.

2

Behind the tall and turreted walls of the palace grounds the Princess paced back and forth in her private garden.

It was a beautiful garden. Peacocks strutted across its smooth green lawns. Fountains sprinkled drops of water like glittering jewels. Lilies, lady slippers, and shooting stars grew among the blue-eyed grasses near the pool. Butterflies—orange and yellow and white and black—fluttered from flower to flower. The air was heady with scents of cinnamon, clove, and apricots. Bright birds sang.

But the Princess walked as if in a trance. Ever since she had gazed into the eyes of the goatherd, she had been unable to think of anyone else. She knew the goatherd was the only man she would ever consent to marry and, by the laws of the kingdom, it was time for her to choose a husband. But she feared her father would not approve of her choice. So the Princess grieved and tears fell from her beautiful eyes.

"Do not cry, dear Princess," the voice of her Fairy Godmother came suddenly out of nowhere.

"Oh, how glad I am to hear you!" cried the unhappy Princess, cheering up a little. "Did you know how much I needed you?"

"I always know when you are sad," said the Fairy Godmother. "It makes my eyes water. In fact, I even know why you are sad. You are thinking of the goatherd. But listen carefully—I have a plan. I have suggested to your father that you will agree to marry the first citizen of Ure to present the Court with a flask of sea water."

"Sea water!" exclaimed the Princess in astonishment, for only members of the Royal

13

Family had ever reached the sea. "Sea water! Oh-h-h, but I wouldn't marry anyone but the goatherd—not if he were to bring me a hundred flasks."

"But if it were the goatherd...?" said the Fairy Godmother and the Princess was quietened by the tone of her voice.

"As I said, I have a plan, but it will succeed only with your help. You must give me your word that you will never for a moment doubt that all will be well in the end, even when things seem to be going very badly or—worse—when nothing seems to be happening at all. This will be more difficult than you think. In fact, there will be times when it will be very difficult indeed. But you must try," said the Fairy Godmother. "It is our only hope."

"Oh, I will!" said the now thoughtful Princess. "With all my heart!"

3

The Kingdom of Ure, you will remember, is a land-locked kingdom and none but members of the Royal Family had ever reached the sea. In fact, many of its inhabitants had never even heard of it. Of those who had, most were not interested, while others thought of it as nothing more than a tale told to rambunctious children—for the sea was reported to say soowish-soowish, a sound known to have a mysterious soothing effect.

Some legends told of travellers who had set out in search of it and never returned; others claimed it teemed with terrifying monsters. And who could seriously believe in something that was variously described as grey, or green, or blue—or as smooth as a millpond, or filled with mountainous peaks?

When the King announced that the Princess would marry the first man to return with a flask of sea water, every unmarried man in the kingdom was eager to compete, for the winner would not only marry the Princess, he would reign with her when the old King died. But after considering the difficulties of the task ahead, many decided that the girl next door had grown remarkably attractive lately and, on second thought, kingly duties would be nothing but a burden and a bore.

Finally, there were only three young men in all the land who resolved to win the Princess—Stabdyl, Mungu and a dusty young goatherd no one had ever seen before who arrived outside the Palace gates just as the announcement was proclaimed.

Stabdyl was well known in Ure. He was the reckless and idle son of one of the King's advisors. He had no wish to marry the Princess or anyone else, but his father, who recognized

the advantage of having the Princess as his daughter in-law, persuaded his son to enter the contest by offering him the fastest horse in the kingdom.

Mungu, vain and ambitious, was stepson of the King's cousin, and his heart was set on the throne. In preparation for the contest, and as befitted one destined to be King, he equipped himself with a fine steed and a mounted servant to carry his belongings—all, that is, but the beautiful cut-glass flask in which to bring back the sea water. That he would carry himself.

The goatherd, dusty and weary, had arrived at the palace gate with a single wish in his heart: to see the Princess one more time. But when he learned that with a flask of sea water he could not only see her again but might even win her hand, he put his mind to work. With what remained of his money, he bought a pair of stout boots for the journey. And because he was far from stupid, he knew he should find out everything he could about the sea before setting forth in search of it. To this end he listened attentively to talk in the town and asked questions whenever possible. But the answers he received were so contradictory that he found himself more confused than before he began. As to where the sea was, or how he would recognize it, nobody knew. Nobody, that is, but the King and the Princess and he could not ask them.

Stabdyl and Mungu set forth from the capital to the waving of flags and the flourish of trumpets. But the goatherd, poor and friendless, had no one to see him off. Nor was he in any great hurry to leave, for if speed were necessary to win the Princess, he—without a horse—was already doomed. So instead of following behind in the dust, he set off for the palace, hoping to catch one final glimpse of the Princess before he left.

No sooner had he arrived outside the palace wall than he saw an old beggar woman who, to his surprise, grabbed him by the arm and pushed him through a small gate.

Inside was a garden unlike anything he had ever seen—green velvet lawns, fruit-laden trees, and birdsong so sweet that he stopped, stock-still, to listen. And then, rounding the corner of a little pavilion, came the Princess herself.

The goatherd's heart skipped a beat and he was quite speechless when he flung himself to his knees at her feet. But the Princess took his hand in hers and bade him stand and as she looked deep into his eyes he saw that her gaze was even bluer and more beautiful than he remembered; and her fingers trembled in his as they stood for a minute or an hour—how could they tell? —before he drew her to him and held her against his breast.

"You must go now," she said at last. "You must delay no longer. But before you go, you must tell me your name."

"I am the goatherd," replied the goatherd.

"No, your name" laughed the Princess. "Herding goats is what you do. What do they call you?"

"They call me the goatherd, or just—Goatherd," he replied, not understanding.

"But you must have a name," she said. "I shall give you one," and she shut her eyes and crinkled her delicious nose in thought. And then, "Galaad," she said. "I shall call you Galaad, because it rhymes with glad. Now go, Galaad, and take this for your journey," and she took from around her neck a golden locket, which she slipped over his head.

"Travel light," she went on, "for it is a long journey. And never doubt that you will find the sea in the end. As to what it is like, I think you will know it when you see it. It is wide as the skies and blue as my eyes." She led him quickly to the little gate, pressed her lips to his and lifted the latch.

The goatherd was once again on the city street, but now he had a name—Galaad—which the Princess had given him, and her beautiful golden locket, and he knew a little bit more about the sea.

4

Stabdyl, when he set out from the capital, travelled east across the rolling plains, for only there could he gallop his horse. In fact, he travelled so fast that at the end of the first day's journey he and his fiery steed were exhausted and could go no further. Stopping at a lonely hut, he asked shelter of the old woman who opened the door.

"Come in, come in," the old woman said. "But your horse is in a lather, fine sir, and I have no servant to rub it down. If you can look after it yourself, I'll be about making your bed and heating some broth for your supper."

"I'm tired, old woman," Stabdyl replied. "Let me eat the soup first and I'll attend to my horse later." And so Stabdyl tied his poor horse to a tree and went inside and greedily drank the soup. Then he fell fast asleep.

When he awoke in the morning and remembered that he had to be first at the sea, he called for his breakfast.

"I have just enough wood to heat the porridge," the old woman said. "Would you split me a few sticks of kindling before you go on your way?"

But Stabdyl was in too great a hurry. He grabbed his porridge and, barely thanking the old woman for her hospitality, saddled his horse, leaped onto its back, and touched his spurs to its ribs. But the fastest horse in the Kingdom stood stock still. Neither spurs nor whip made the least difference.

Enraged, Stabdyl jumped to the ground and pulled on the bridle but pull as he would, the horse refused to budge. "All right, then," he cried in rage. "Stay where you are, I'll go on foot."

Before long he discovered that his beautiful boots, handsomely tooled and fine in stirrups, were ill-suited to walking. In no time at all, his feet were blistered and sore and he had to sit down and bathe them in a stream.

"More haste, less speed, Stabdyl," said a small voice nearby.

Stabdyl looked around but all he could see were the beady little eyes of a field mouse. Now Stabdyl knew perfectly well that mice can't talk but as he stared at this one he saw quite clearly that the voice was coming from its tiny mouth. Nevertheless, he said, "Mice can't talk."

"Of course not," said the mouse.

"Then why are you talking?"

"Just passing the time of day, as a courteous field mouse should," the mouse replied.

"Do you live around here?" Stabdyl inquired.

"Around here, around there," answered the mouse, gesturing widely.

"Then perhaps," said Stabdyl eagerly, "you have seen the sea in your travels."

"Indeed," said the field mouse, "and of course."

"Could you—lead me to it?" asked Stabdyl, getting to his feet.

"I could," said the field mouse.

"Then let us make haste," said Stabdyl. He had forgotten his sore feet.

"I said I could, I didn't say I would." The mouse came close to Stabdyl. "In fact," he began, whereupon he ran fearlessly up Stabdyl's trouser leg and disappeared into the pouch that hung from Stabdyl's belt. From there the rest of the mouse's sentence sounded like nothing more than so much squeaking, which Stabdyl couldn't understand at all.

Stabdyl grew impatient. "I am in a great hurry," he said, speaking into his pouch. "A very GREAT HURRY. And if, as you say, you know the way to the sea, then take me to it. There is no time to lose."

"Time to lose?" said the field mouse, popping his head over the edge of the pouch. "Who ever heard of losing time? Here we find time. We never lose it."

"It must have been lost once in order for you to find it," Stabdyl retorted, drawn into the argument in spite of himself. And then, becoming impatient, "If you're so good at finding time, then please be kind enough to find enough to take me to the sea."

"We shall have to look for it then," said the field mouse calmly. "Would you be so good as to help?" And he ran down Stabdyl's leg and began peering behind rocks in a quite methodical way.

"The larger rocks," he said, "you can handle better than I, and I'd be greatly obliged…"

Stabdyl was near the end of his politeness but he couldn't afford to lose his guide to the sea and so he began, with not very good grace, to move the large rocks and look under them.

"Do you usually find time under rocks?" he asked.

"As a matter of fact," said the mouse, continuing his search, "it has never been found there before. But you simply don't know where you'll find it next. Here one day, there another."

Just as Stabdyl had decided he would do better to go on his way alone, the field mouse squeaked, "Eureka! A good-sized piece! What luck! Quite enough to take us to the sea, if we hurry." And with that he set off at a quick, skittering run.

Following him proved difficult, for the mouse could go where Stabdyl could not. At times Stabdyl thought he had lost the mouse entirely. But finally, after many detours, disappearances, and reunions, the mouse cried out, "We're getting close!"

Stabdyl strained his ears for the soowish-soowish the old tales had led him to expect, but all he could hear were sucking sounds made by his bare feet in marshy ground. Yet he began to be excited at the thought of reaching the sea and he felt grateful to the mouse. Then he congratulated himself on how clever he had been and before long he had convinced himself that his success was due entirely to his own resourcefulness and skill. And he saw himself winning the hand of the Princess and leading a life of luxury and leisure, his stables filled with the finest horses. But to the Princess herself he gave no thought at all.

"We'll just about make it," cried the mouse, breaking into Stabdyl's reverie.

"Make what?"

"Make it to the sea, of course," the mouse said as patiently as possible. "I only found a medium-sized piece of time, you know, and what with your slowness and one thing and another, I began to wonder if we would."

At that moment they came out from a clump of swamp alder and "Voila!" cried the mouse, gesturing with a rather muddy paw.

Stabdyl looked across the wide expanse of shallow water, at the reeds and rushes growing at its edges, at the pink and yellow lilies floating on its smooth surface. Then, heart pounding in his chest, hand shaking with excitement, Stabdyl stooped and carefully filled his flask.

5

Having watched Stabdyl gallop eastward, Mungu, accompanied by his mounted servant, spurred his own steed and turned its head to the west. His plan was to ride directly to the high mountains from whose topmost crests he believed he would be able to see the sea.

When darkness fell, Mungu's servant pitched a fine silken tent for his master to sleep in. At dawn they broke camp and worked their horses up the dangerous rocky track. A week passed in this manner. It grew colder as they climbed. The air became harder to breathe. Their horses moved more and more slowly.

One day the servant, who was an old man, could go no further. Mungu gave him orders to return home on foot.

Astride his own horse, his servant's poor beast now loaded with all his possessions, Mungu struggled on. Had it not been for his dream of the crown, he could not have borne such hardship.

At length, weary—and hungry too, for his food was running low—he came to the high pass from which he hoped to have a distant view of the sea. But dense cloud filled the air and he could see no more than a few yards ahead of him. Mungu was about to force his horses on when he noticed a cave in the rock and within it, sitting as if carved, was an extraordinary figure. His hair and beard were white as icicles. In one hand he held a shell—something Mungu had never seen before—and his eyes, the only part of him that looked alive, blazed like blue fire.

Apart from his horses and the occasional mountain goat, Mungu had seen no living thing for several days, so he stared at the figure as if it were a vision. Then in the silence and out of his terrible loneliness Mungu said, "I am tired and I am cold and I am looking for the sea."

"The Western Sea?" the old man inquired. "You are a long way from the sea, my son."

"How far?" asked Mungu.

"Farther than you think," the old man said.

"Old man," said Mungu and his voice was hard, "I have to reach the sea. If you know where it is and how far away it is, perhaps you can give me some help."

"I could give you help," the old man replied, "but I don't think you would accept it."

"I must reach the sea!" said Mungu again.

"Very well," said the old man. "I have three pieces of advice. The first, that you leave your horses with me."

"Leave my horses!" shouted Mungu. "But my horses are my only means of transportation."

"The second," went on the old man as if Mungu had not spoken, "that you leave your saddle-bags with me."

"Never!" Cried Mungu. "My saddle-bags hold everything I own, including my beautiful cut-glass flask in which to carry home the sea water."

"And third," said the old man, "that you leave your cut-glass flask."

"You would be happy to own all my belongings, wouldn't you, you ragged old beggar," cried Mungu in a fury. "You could sell my horses and my silken tent and my golden dishes and my beautiful cut-glass flask, couldn't you? No, old man. I am not such a fool as you think."

But suddenly the old man didn't look like a beggar at all. His ragged clothing gave off a blinding light, his eyes shone like frosty stars and Mungu's blood froze in his veins. He was more afraid than he had ever been in his life before and he urged his horses on.

That night, as Mungu was camped on a narrow ledge—too narrow for him to pitch his silken tent—his fine horse missed its footing in the dark and dropped down the sheer face of the mountain.

"Oh, clumsy horse! Oh, careless, stupid horse!" cried Mungu in a fury, clenching his fists and shaking them at the stars. "What am I going to do?"

Fearful that his other horse might meet the same fate, taking all his possessions with it, Mungu in desperation, decided to carry the saddle-bags himself. Burdened now by his many belongings which grew heavier and heavier, stumbling often, nearly falling, he and his servant's horse picked their way down the narrow, rocky trail.

Mungu soon found that it was impossible to continue in this way. Reluctantly, he began throwing his things away. First to go was his beautiful silken tent; next his golden dishes; then his purple velvet cloak, his green brocade trousers, his richly tooled boots, and the many lengths of coloured silks to tie his turbans. But Mungu's heart was heavy and the steep slope down which he struggled was slippery and treacherous in the rain.

Then one morning, when Mungu had almost forgotten the sun, he awakened to its light. For the first time since crossing the height of land he could see more than a few feet ahead of him. Anxiously he searched the horizon for the sea, but all he could see were rolling foothills, rolling forever and ever.

Mungu remembered the words of the old man in the cave: "You are a long way from the sea, my son." And he began to wonder, as many of his countrymen had before him, if the sea were no more than a fable, after all.

But the dream of being King drove him on.

By the time he reached the grasslands, Mungu had nothing but his horse, the clothes he stood up in, and his beautiful cut-glass flask. The horse he decided to leave behind. After so terrible a journey it was mere skin and bone. He would make better time on foot.

At night, with nothing to shelter him from the weather, he lay down under the stars. His sight became sharp from looking for wild berries and there was a crazed look in his eyes. He grew thin and strong as steel and, as he walked on in search of the sea, he made plans for when he would be King. His plans would not have pleased the citizens of Ure.

Then, one day when he was bending over a rushing stream to drink, his beautiful cut-glass flask slipped from his bag and was dashed to pieces on the rocks.

For the first time in his long, hard journey, Mungu sank down in despair and buried his head in his hands.

6

Galaad, if you remember, set out from the capital of Ure with a light heart. He wore the Princess's locket around his neck and her words still rang in his ears.

Like Stabdyl before him, he set off towards the east. And like Stabdyl, he too, came to the hut of the old woman, who made him soup and gave him a bed. It was the first bed Galaad had slept in since leaving his own village so he awakened refreshed and grateful.

"What can I do for you in return for your hospitality, Mother?" Galaad asked after breakfast.

"Oh, young master, if you could split me some wood," the old woman said, "for truly, I am past it."

And so Galaad set to and split a large pile of wood. And when he had stacked it neatly and was about to go on his way, the old woman said, "And if you could draw me some water, young master, I would be very pleased."

And so Galaad set to and drew seven buckets of water, one for each day of the week. And when he had finished the old woman said, "Young master, it's a long time since anyone has passed this way with a willing heart and who knows when anyone will again—and my roof is badly in need of repair."

And so Galaad set to and mended the roof and filled the floor boards and the cracks around the doors and windows until at last the house was as snug as a house can be. And when he had finished, the old woman said, "You have looked after me like a son. Go now, and may success go with you."

And then she reached into her apron pocket and brought forth a smooth stone—as black and as shiny as the Princess's hair. "Take this," she said and she put it in his palm where it lay heavy for its size, and warm. "It was given to me many years ago and it is said to grant one wish to each owner. I never used it until last week when I wished for a strong young man who would look after me as if he were my son. Today it granted my wish. Now, it is yours. Use it only when all else fails."

Galaad put the stone in his pouch, embraced the old woman and went on his way with a light heart.

Before he had gone very far he heard a small voice saying, "Are you looking for the sea, too?" And there was a field mouse sitting on a log.

"Too?" asked Galaad. "Have there been others?"

"One other," the mouse replied. "And I took him to the sea and he filled a bottle with water to win the hand of a Princess. But why would he want a bottle of sea water, I can't imagine."

Galaad's heart fell. If someone had been to the sea before him, what point was there in going on? But at the thought of the Princess he knew he must never give up.

"Would you take me to the sea?" he asked the mouse. "Now?"

"Willingly," the mouse replied. And once again he led the way along the stream until they came to the same expanse of water with reeds and rushes growing at its edges and water lilies floating on its smooth surface.

"As wide as the skies and as blue as her eyes," Galaad said to himself. And it did, indeed, seem to fit the description. Almost, that is. It was not quite as wide as the skies but it was a large body of water, larger than any that Galaad had ever seen.

As he bent down to fill his goatskin he said to himself, "If I return with all speed, perhaps I can still arrive first at the Palace." And thanking the mouse for his help Galaad began the journey back to the capital.

Almost at once he came across a man sitting by the roadside. "Water. Water," the man croaked, pointing to his mouth. So Galaad unstoppered his goatskin and handed it to the thirsty man who drank and drank and drank until there was no drop left.

"Are you better, Father?" Galaad inquired. "Because, if so, I must return to the sea to refill my goatskin, for without sea water I cannot win the hand of the Princess whom I love."

"Sea water!" laughed the man. "Where do you come from, boy, that you think that was sea water? Why, no one can drink sea water. It's too salty."

"Salty?" Said Galaad and his eyes widened and his heart lightened.

"Salty as a kipper," the man said cheerfully. "Salty as an anchovy."

Galaad who had never heard of either kippers or anchovies asked, just to make absolutely certain, "As salty as—salt?"

"If you wish," said the man. "As salty as salt. As salty as tears."

"As wide as the skies, as blue as her eyes, and as salty as tears. It's not a very good rhyme," Galaad said, "but it does help with the description."

The man took from his pouch a beautiful shell, such as Galaad had never seen, and he held it to Galaad's ear so that he could hear the soowish-soowish of the sea.

"As wide as the skies, and blue as her eyes, as salty as tears, and with shells on its shores," the man said, adding, "And it's no great distance from here at all, at all, the sea isn't. Why, this road you're on leads directly to it."

So, once again, grateful and full of thanks, Galaad set off in search of the sea.

7

Meanwhile, in the Kingdom of Ure, husbands told wives and wives told children that Stabdyl was on his way home with a flask of sea water. So fast, in fact, did the news travel that it reached the capital ahead of Stabdyl himself. And great was the rejoicing, for everyone looked forward to the celebrations which accompany a royal wedding...everyone, that is, but the Princess, who was finding it very hard to remember that all would be well in the end.

Outside the palace an excited crowd awaited the arrival of Stabdyl. And when, at last, he appeared—bathed, scented, and dressed in his finest clothes, with the sea water in its silver flask carried on a velvet cushion—a joyous cry arose to greet him.

Inside the palace the King sat on his golden throne; by his side sat the Princess, deathly pale; and, more than usually prominent, the King's advisor, father of Stabdyl, who already thought of the Princess as his daughter-in-law.

Stabdyl, with barely a glance at the Princess, his mind on fire with the dream of fast horses, stepped forward and presented his flask to the King. To the astonishment of the Court, the King unstoppered the flask and put it to his lips as if to drink it.

"This is not sea water," the King said.

"Not sea water!" cried the King's advisor, his voice quavering.

"But, your majesty," protested Stabdyl, "I filled this flask with my own hands. From the sea itself."

"What makes you think it was the sea?" the King inquired.

"I travelled many miles," Stabdyl replied. "Miles and miles with no sight of the sea. Then, when I had nearly given up hope, I met a mouse. He led me to the sea.

"A mouse?" asked the King and all the courtiers echoed their Monarch. "A mouse?" "A mou-ouse?" "A MOUse!" "A MOUSE!"

"A mouse," Stabdyl repeated, feeling now rather foolish.

"I think it may be generally assumed," said the King, "that if a mouse leads you to the sea, it will be a mouse's sea, not a man's. This water, I conclude, is from a pond. Possibly one with reeds and rushes growing at its edges and lilies floating where its shallows are."

Anyone watching the King's advisor would have seen the colour leave his cheeks at these words. And anyone watching the Princess would have seen the colour return to hers.

As for Stabdyl, he felt a pang of disappointment as the fast horses of which he had dreamed, slipped from his grasp. But he was not one to waste time on regrets. Already he was thinking of other ways to amuse himself.

8

Galaad, now sure of his way, followed the road the man said led directly to the sea. He knew that he had been saved from returning to the Court with a goatskin of pond water. But what he did not know was that he was crossing lands owned by the Wizard of the Eastern Seaboard.

He had travelled no distance at all before storm clouds filled the sky and the bright day darkened. Lightning crackled overhead, distant thunder rolled. Rain came down in sheets. A nearby house offered promise of shelter and when Galaad knocked on its door, a servant answered.

"May I take shelter from the rain?" Galaad asked. "It's a bad time to be out on foot."

"My master does not like visitors," the servant replied. "But he is away on business and I could do with a bit of human company."

He led Galaad down a long dark corridor. Behind shut doors on either side Galaad could hear dogs barking and cats meowing and horses neighing and goats bleating. He had worked too long as a goatherd not to know an unhappy goat when he heard one. And he didn't think the other animals sounded too happy either.

"What a lot of animals your master owns," said Galaad.

"Aye," replied the servant, "that he does. And I reckon he will own one more by night-fall."

Then he ushered Galaad into the kitchen and took his wet clothes and gave him a steaming cup of mead, sweet and soothing. Galaad drank it gratefully and slipped off at once into a deep sleep.

"Ha ha!" said the Wizard returning home, "has my good servant caught another human being with his honey? Has he indeed! What shall we turn him into, my man? I've not done a goat for a very long time. I think I'll turn him into a goat."

The Wizard was a tall man in a long coat with trailing sleeves and eyes as black as liquorice.

"Thinks he can cross my land, does he?" he asked of the air as he passed his fingers over and around the sleeping Galaad.

"On second thought," he went on and his fingers traced a slower and more complicated design, "I think I'll make him into a goatherd. He can look after my goats."

He began a jerky dance around Galaad and his voice became cold and hard as he said: "You will forget everything that has ever happened to you. Abracadabra. You will forget your own name and your own mission. Abracadabra. All you will know are my goats. Forever... and ever... and ever."

And such was the power of the Wizard's spell that Galaad indeed forgot everything. He forgot that he was in search of the sea. He forgot his own name. He even forgot the Princess.

9

Now the Wizard was interested in Galaad for political reasons. He had long been an enemy of the King of Ure who refused to make war with him against neighbouring states. So when he had heard that the Princess was about to marry, he made it a point to find out everything he could about the three suitors.

Stabdyl, he discovered, was a greedy and idle boy, always in a hurry and of no conceivable use to him. Galaad clearly would follow in the footsteps of the old King and so he must not be allowed to marry the Princess. But Mungu was vain and ambitious and greedy and cruel, just the kind of accomplice the Wizard needed.

With Stabdyl out of the running and Galaad busy with the goats, the Wizard could give his full attention to Mungu. Not that it was going to prove as easy as he'd hoped, for Mungu was on the other side of the continent, wandering half-crazed in the direction of the Western Sea—a region where the Wizard's powers were greatly reduced. Although he could assist Mungu in bringing about Mungu's own desires, he was completely unable to put ideas or wishes in Mungu's head. And the trouble with Mungu at the moment was that he had fallen into a terrible aimlessness and only at times remembered why he had set out on his endless journey. So all the Wizard could do was wait.

Then one morning Mungu awakened and thought of the flask of sea water, without which his dream could never come true. And he thought of the Western Sea which the old man in the cave had spoken of those many long months ago. And no sooner had the thought entered his mind than the Wizard deposited him on its golden shore.

Dazed, Mungu stared at the sweep of blue water, vaster and more blue than anything he had ever imagined. Then he fell on his knees and tried to drink, but the salt on his lips and throat was like fire and he ran back from the sea as if burned and once again he forgot the crown, and the Wizard could only wait.

When at last Mungu realized that this water was, in fact, the very sea for which he had been searching, he was desperate to find a container, fill it, and return to the Kingdom of Ure with all speed. So the Wizard, invisible as air, directed Mungu to a stoppered bottle which lay, half-hidden in a tangle of seaweed.

Now everyone knows that a stoppered bottle may well contain a genie—everyone, that is, but Mungu who, with only one idea in his head and no thought at all of possible consequences, pulled on the stopper with all his strength.

In a flash, an immense figure rose like smoke from the bottle, towering over the astonished Mungu and frightening him half to death. But to his surprise, the ferocious-looking creature bowed low and said in a voice so loud Mungu had to put his hands over his ears, "Command me!"

Without hesitation, eyes blazing, greed bursting through his heart, Mungu cried out in a great voice, almost a match for the genie's, "Make me King!"

10

The Wizard was well content with the spell he had put on Galaad, for Galaad had forgotten everything. Day after day he took the Wizard's goats to pasture and night after night he brought them home again. No thought of the Princess or the sea ever entered his head. And so he might have gone on forever had he not met the same old woman who had pushed him into the Princess's garden. Not that he recognized her. The Wizard had seen to that.

"Young man," she begged, "I am poor and you are rich. Give me one of your goats."

"I am sorry, Mother," Galaad replied. "I can't give you a goat, for the goats are not mine. I am only a poor goatherd with nothing to give you at all."

"How can I believe what you tell me when you wear that beautiful golden locket around your neck?"

"Golden locket?" said Galaad, who had forgotten all about it. "I have no locket." But when he put his hand to his neck he found that he had.

"If those goats are not yours, the locket is. You could give me the locket," the old woman said.

"Old woman," Galaad replied, "I wish I could give you something that would be of use to you. But I cannot give you the locket."

"You don't care about a poor old woman at all," she whined. "Why can't you give it to me, if it is yours?"

Now Galaad didn't know why he couldn't give her the locket. All he knew was that it gave him a feeling so sweet, so half-forgotten, that he wanted nothing more than to hold it in his hand and stare at it.

"How is it that a poor goatherd can own a golden locket?" the old woman went on, sidling up to him and looking at him suspiciously. "Perhaps," she said, "you stole it. Heh-heh-heh." And she laughed a nasty laugh.

"Oh, no," said Galaad horrified. "I didn't steal it." But poor Galaad was not even certain of that, for there was nothing but a blank in his head when he tried to remember where it came from.

"Aha!" the old woman exclaimed as she took the locket in her hand and turned it over, "you must have stolen it right enough. And from the Princess, too. See, here is the Royal Seal."

"The Princess?" cried Galaad and his heart leaped. "The Princess? What Princess, old woman?"

"The Princess of Ure who, at this very moment, is expecting one of her suitors to return with a flask of sea water."

"Sea water!" said Galaad. And as he uttered those words the spell broke. All memory came rushing back. He remembered the mountain meadows outside his village and the first glimpse he had had of the Princess; he remembered his meeting with the Princess in the garden when she gave him his name and her locket. He remembered his search for the sea. And he knew that what he should be doing now was continuing that search and not wasting time on goats and old women—for Galaad didn't realize that this was the same old woman who had helped him before and that it was thanks to her that the Wizard's spell was now undone.

"You must excuse me, Mother," said Galaad. "I have just remembered something very important."

"Not so fast, not so fast," the old woman cautioned. "You are planning to go to the sea. But if you abandon the goats the Wizard, under whose spell you have been, will know at once that you are free of it. On his land he is a powerful magician and can cast a spell stronger than stone."

Galaad looked at the old woman in amazement. How did she know that he was planning to go to the sea?

"You are wondering if I can read your mind," she went on. "Well, I can. Now listen. I have a plan. Go home tonight as usual. Then tomorrow morning when you take your goats to pasture, drive them due east without stopping. By midday you should be at the sea. Fill your goatskin with sea water and walk south along the shore. On the shore you are safe. Below the high-tide mark the Wizard has no power over you. You will come, at last, to a great headland jutting into the ocean, and here you will have to be extremely careful, for this headland cannot be climbed. From there, the only way to Ure is across the

Wizard's land. It is not a long way but it is full of dangers. You will have to have all your wits about you for this last part of the journey."

Suddenly it came to Galaad that this was the same old woman who had helped him before. "Who are you, old woman?" he asked. But he asked the question of the air. The old woman had disappeared as if she had never been.

11

Galaad did as the old woman advised. He drove his goats home to the Wizard's house in the evening, ate his bread and water, and went to bed in the stable. When morning broke, he was already on his way due east. And as the sun stood at mid-point in the sky, Galaad smelled a totally new smell—tangy and delicious and invigorating; and mounting a low sandy hillock, he saw before him, "wide as the skies and blue as her eyes" what could only be the sea. Sparkling sapphire water stretched in three directions and where it met the shore it broke in foam as white as the lace at the neck and wrists of the Princess's dress. And where the foam dissolved and disappeared in the sand, it left an irregular line of glistening shells.

With a loud cry that drove his goats forward, Galaad raced into the healing waves and in his heart there was no doubt at all that he had, at last, arrived at the sea. And it was more beautiful even than he had dreamed.

Then above the *soowish-soowish* of its waters he heard great joyful cries and, turning, he saw that the goats had changed into young men and women who came splashing towards him, calling out their thanks that they were free of the goat bodies into which the Wizard had locked them.

And then Galaad remembered the Princess. He bent and filled his goatskin with sea water, and as he did so it changed to a beautiful golden flask. And he saw that his clothing too, instead of being the simple homespun of a goatherd, was changed into velvets and brocades like the garments of a prince.

But the advice of the old woman sounded in his ears and he called to his new-found companions to follow him, warning them that they were only safe from the enchantments of the Wizard if they stayed below the high-tide line.

"Keep close together and follow me," he cautioned as they stopped to pick up shells, to make chains of seaweed, or to play in the sparkling waters. Once or twice he was tempted to go on without them but each time a heavy weight fell upon his heart and he knew that he must take them with him.

And so, with many stops and starts, they travelled on together until they arrived at the great unscalable headland where they must cross the Wizard's land. And Galaad knew that of all the trials he had so far faced, this—because he knew about it in advance—was the worst. He called his friends together and warned them of the dangers ahead.

What he saw, when he climbed a high rock to survey the Wizard's land, was a flower-filled meadow, golden in the late afternoon sun—as innocent-appearing a meadow as you could wish to see. And beyond, at no great distance, the majestic mountains of Ure.

While he stood, considering the time it would take them to reach the mountains, one of the young men ran up from the sands, hand outstretched, to pick a wild rose. But just as he picked it from the bush, he was a goat again. And all the young men and women on the shore cried out in fear of the Wizard.

Then Galaad remembered the stone that could grant him one wish and he pulled it from his pouch. Holding it firmly in his fist and thinking fast but very carefully, he wished: "Carry us all safely to the Kingdom of Ure—including the goat."

No sooner had he spoken than it was as if they were lifted in the folds of an invisible cloak and carried high into the air, skirts and shirt-tails and hair blowing out about them and the poor goat bleating pitifully as he tipped and tilted in his sudden flight.

In no more time than it takes to tell, they arrived safely in the Kingdom of Ure. Galaad, stopping only to bathe and brush the sand from his hair, took his beautiful golden flask of sea water to the Palace where he presented it to the King. And when the King had put it to his lips to make sure it was truly sea water, he gave Galaad the Princess's hand in marriage.

For the wedding everyone wore their best clothes and there was a great feast and the dancing continued for weeks. Next to the Princess, the most beautiful of all was the Fairy Godmother, dressed at last in her rightful clothes of gossamer and looking almost as young as the Princess herself. But whenever Galaad looked into her eyes, he couldn't help being reminded of the old woman who had helped him in his travels—and of the old man.

12

And Mungu? Mungu was so greedy to be King, if you remember, and in so great a hurry, that he forgot to ask the genie to make him the King of Ure. And the only Kingdom without a King at the moment he made his wish was a rocky, wind-swept island a thousand miles away. And there Mungu is monarch and he thinks and he thinks.

And the goat? Oh, yes, the goat! But that is another story.

THE GOAT THAT FLEW

Once upon a time there was a goat that flew. As to why he flew, or how, he hadn't the least idea. He had no wings, not even a magic carpet, yet there he was, high in the sky, tipping and tilting in a way that made his poor head giddy.

Then, as he got the hang of it, he began to enjoy the sensation. Wind whistled through his whiskers. Treetops whizzed by. He thought he was a bird. He even tried to sing. But, alas, when he opened his mouth, the same old bleat came out.

His landing was a disaster.

Crash, bang, bump and a tangle of legs.

At first he just lay there—a bag of bones. Then he wiggled each ankle in turn to see if it were broken and wondered about his horns. And then—very carefully—he stood up. A dozen pairs of goat eyes were staring at him like twenty-four yellow marbles.

The oldest Billy stepped forward and bleated at the top of his lungs, "Where have you come from?"

The goat that flew couldn't remember.

"Bleat up! Bleat up!" the old Billy said. "No manners at all." And then, very loudly, as if the goat that flew were deaf, "The least you can do is tell us your name."

But the goat that flew couldn't remember his name, either. "What?" he wondered to himself, and "Who?" but no name came to him. "I—I forget," he said.

"You forget?" cried the old Billy. "What do you mean, you forget? No one forgets his name! We shall have to call you Forgetter."

Then the twelve goats crowded closer. "Teach us to fly," they said. But Forgetter hadn't the least idea how.

Now, as is the way with goats, some thought this meant he refused to teach them, while others thought he was standoffish and stuck-up. And when he tried to explain that he didn't know how to fly, they thought he was a liar as well.

Day after day Forgetter stood on a hilltop, made himself feel as light as possible, lifted one hoof, then another, and flapped his hairy ears. "If I could fly once," he thought, "why can't I fly again?" But he couldn't.

One morning, when he was feeling particularly lonely, he chanced to meet an ancient and wise Billy, whose white beard fell down to his knees. "I am the Venerable William," the old Billy said. "I've heard about you, my boy. You're the flier, aren't you? But one flight does not a flyer make and goats aren't made for flying. No wings," he said, and gave a little skip.

There was something so kindly about the Venerable William that Forgetter was soon pouring out his heart. "How shall I ever find a friend?" he asked.

"There are many more goats in Ure than the ones around here, you know," the Venerable William soothed. "Why, there are all spots and stripes of goats for you to meet. And do you know that on the other side of the mountain there are goats who are actually owned by people and spend their whole lives doing what people wish? No freedom at all. What you need to do is travel, my boy. Get new air in your nostrils. See the world."

And so Forgetter, still lonely but none the less grateful, set out to see the world.

Many and remarkable were the sights he saw. He did, indeed, see goats who were owned by people but he certainly didn't want people to own him! He saw mountain ranges with snow on their peaks and flower-filled meadows and wide river valleys and vast, dark forests and glittering lakes, and—almost impossible for him to believe—he saw villages full of people, where there were no goats at all. After many days of watching from a safe distance, he came to the astonishing conclusion that there was more to the world than goats.

And so Forgetter began to think less about goats and more about people, until his thoughts finally led him to the capital of Ure.

It was a busy city and he was confused by the crowded streets where his hooves made a clatter on the cobblestones. As for people, they had little time for him—unless, that is, he reached up to eat a mouthful of leaves from a branch overhead, or nibbled a tender shoot from a flowering shrub. Then they shouted, "Gaar!" or "Shoo!" and shoved him aside. Sometimes they even gave him a passing kick for good measure. And the language they spoke was one he could make no sense of at all.

One day when he was thirsty and tired and more lonely than ever he came to a high stone wall, too high to see over—even when he stood on his hind legs.

A great curiosity filled Forgetter.

He had to know what lay on the other side of that wall.

He wanted to rest, but something drew him on and on, and on and on until at last he reached an open work-gate. Peering through it Forgetter saw a garden more beautiful than anything he could have imagined. He longed to drink from its splashing fountain, to lie down in the shade of its trees. And as he gazed, a beautiful girl approached, opened a gate, and put her hand on his head.

"I hope you will be happy here," she said.

Forgetter could hardly believe his ears. She was actually speaking his language.

"Why," he said, astonished, "you speak Goat!"

"Not very good Goat," the girl replied apologetically.

"But I could teach you," said Forgetter eagerly, for now he had forgotten how tired he was, he had even changed his mind about people, and he wanted to stay in that garden forever. "I could give you lessons. Go on, say something—any old thing will do—and I'll correct you if you're wrong."

The girl spoke slowly and carefully. "I was a goat once," she said.

Forgetter laughed and laughed. "You were never a goat," he said "What you mean is that you had a goat once."

"You remind me of my friend," she went on.

"No, no, no!" said Forgetter, laughing again. "Wrong word. What you mean is, I remind you of your goat."

The girl shook her head as if she knew something he didn't and gave him a loving pat. Forgetter had never felt so happy.

That night he dreamed a wonderful dream. He dreamed he was a man. He had black hair and blue eyes, hands instead of hooves and a beautiful pair of satin trousers. So when he wakened in the morning and saw his goat body, it was doubly hard to bear. And when the girl joined him in the garden he said, "Last night I dreamed I was a man." Then he fell silent. Thinking. An important question was worrying him. "When you said you were a goat once, did you mean that you dreamed you were a goat?" he asked.

"No," said the girl. "That's not what I meant at all." And then, changing the subject, "Tell me your name."

Forgetter felt foolish. "Because I can't remember it, they call me Forgetter."

"I," said the girl, "shall call you Erland. After my friend. His name was Erland."

"Erland?" said Forgetter, and he felt the most extraordinary sensation in his heart or his head. "And yours?" he asked.

"Corille," she replied. "Difficult for a goat to pronounce, I think."

And she was right. Try as he would, Forgetter couldn't get his tongue around it. But what a tinkle of bells when she said it. Corille. Corille. Corille.

He felt a great surge of excitement as if he were on the brink of something very important. But he couldn't make sense of the thoughts in his head.

Corille. Corille. Corille. Somehow the sound made him remember a long-forgotten day when he, Forgetter was not a goat, but a man.

Suddenly he blurted out, "Were we picking berries?"

"Oh, Erland!" cried Corille. "You've remembered! We had wandered on to the Wizard's Land without knowing it. And at once, the sky became black. Black!"

"Did we come to a house?" Forgetter was excited.

"The Wizard's house," said Corille and her eyes were shining.

Forgetter could hardly believe what she was saying. He reared up on his hind legs, as goats do when they are happy, and butted Corille very gently with his horns. "Was I a man? Was I really a man?" he asked, unbelieving.

And then Corille, in a rush, told him how the Wizard had changed them all into goats and put them in the care of a goatherd named Galaad, who had led them to the sea.

"The sea!" said Forgetter, and he gave a long, satisfied bleat. "I remember the sea. How could I have forgotten the sea?"

"It was the sea," Corille went on, "that broke the Wizard's spell. We all ran into the sea and became—ourselves again. The Wizard had no power below the high tide line."

"And then what happened?" Forgetter asked.

"We came to the Wizard's Land. It was beautiful—all covered with flowers—and you raced onto it to pick me a rose." She laid a loving hand on Forgetter's rough head. "Then," Corille shuddered at the memory, "right before our eyes you were turned back into a goat again."

"I remember the rose," said Forgetter. "But why didn't I go into the sea again?" He looked puzzled. "That was all I had to do, wasn't it—go into the sea?"

"There wasn't time," explained Corille. She heaved a great sigh. "Galaad had to hurry back to Ure as he was trying to win the hand of Princess Meera. And he had a magic stone which lifted us across the Wizard's Land so the Wizard couldn't touch us. We rose up into the sky like a flight of birds."

"Oh-h-h!" Said Forgetter. "So that's why I flew. A magic stone! No wonder I could never fly again."

They were both quiet for a long time. And then Forgetter said, "I am Erland. I remember now." And he looked at his goat body and with all his heart he wished to be free of it.

"I must go to the sea," said Forgetter.

Corille shook her head. "Too dangerous. You can only get to the sea by crossing the Wizard's Land. We must think of something else."

And so they thought and they thought.

"I know!" said Corille excitedly. "Prince Galaad brought back a flask of sea water— that's what he had to do to win the hand of Princess Meera...."

And so Corille ran to the palace. When Prince Galaad heard the news of Erland, he was so happy that he pressed the precious flask into her hands.

Corille raced back to the garden. "Oh, Erland! Look! But do stand still. It's not a very big flask and there isn't much water. I mustn't spill a drop." Her hands were shaking as she took the stopper from the beautiful golden flask.

"Are you sure it's sea water?" Erland asked.

"If you want proof—here—sea water's salty." She very carefully poured a little into the palm of her hand for Erland to taste.

"Salty," he nodded happily.

"Erland!" Corille jumped for joy. "You spoke like a human, not a goat."

"So I did," said Erland, astonished. And then, remembering how difficult he had found it to say her name, he said, "Corille." It was perfectly easy. "Corille, Corille, Corille."

"Shut your eyes," commanded Corille and she sprinkled water from the flask onto his eyelids. "Now open them."

"Oh, Erland! Your eyes are blue. Not yellow goat eyes anymore."

"Now my face," said Erland, excited. And, eager to see his face again, she upended the flask.

But alas, not a drop fell out. Although she shook it and shook it there was no water left.

"I am surely worse off," said Erland, in the voice of a despondent young man. "Before, I was an ordinary goat. Now I am a freak—a blue-eyed goat with the voice of a man—fit only for a circus."

"Dear Erland," cried Corille. "I shall look after you here forever. I shall have a special house made for you in the garden and...."

But Erland would hear of no such thing. "I must go back to the sea," he said.

"Oh, Erland," there were tears in Corille's eyes as she spoke, "I am so glad to have found you. Please don't leave me. In the morning we'll talk to Prince Galaad. He'll know what to do. Now, we must sleep."

But Erland couldn't sleep. "I must go to the sea, and I must go tonight," he decided. "Tomorrow may be too late."

And so, as the stars blinked overhead in the night sky, Erland gave a long last look in the direction of Corille's house before he slipped quietly out of the garden and set out for the sea.

Ever since Forgetter had come tumbling out of the blue, the Wizard had watched him with his long-distance eye—the eye that made it possible for him to see anywhere in the world. And the Wizard did not like what he saw.

When the Venerable William had put ideas about travelling into Forgetter's head, the Wizard was angry. When Forgetter had dreamed he was a man, the Wizard became angrier still. And when Corille had reminded Forgetter that he was really Erland, the Wizard fell into a storming rage. He had made Erland a goat once, he had made Erland a goat twice, and a goat Erland was going to stay! When the Wizard saw Corille with the flask of sea water, he roared with fury.

"AAARGH!" he roared, and again "AAARGH!"and the leaves on the trees trembled as if a wind were blowing.

But as long as Erland remained in the Kingdom of Ure, the Wizard was powerless. His magic could not work beyond his own land. So all he had been able to do was await the day when Forgetter would innocently place his fore-hoof over the invisible border.

And now Forgetter was on his way to the sea, and before very long he would be forced to step onto the Wizard's Land.

And when he did, then—then—Forgetter would find out who was in charge. Anticipating that moment, the Wizard rubbed his sandpapery palms together and gave a mean, mirthless laugh.

The first night of Erland's travels, the air was cool and the sky was brilliant with stars. The constellation Schooner shone directly overhead and Erland decided to follow the star in its prow—not that he knew where it pointed, but until he was sure of the way to the sea, it would prevent him from going in circles.

"If I were a true goat," he thought, "I might reach the sea unnoticed. And if I were a man—despite the dangers on the Wizard's Land—I might still get to the sea. So, I shall travel only by night."

As morning dawned he saw that he was on a vast moor stretching in all directions. The only sign of shelter was a little copse uncomfortably close to a small tumble-down cottage. Though the cottage looked abandoned, he approached it with great caution, for fear of waking chickens or a dog.

He chose what he hoped was a safe spot under a tree in the tall grasses and there he settled down for his day's sleep.

A jab in the ribs jarred him awake and a man's harsh voice asked, "What have we here? A stray beast?" And then, as Erland opened his eyes, the man let out a great cry of astonishment. "Ai-ee—ee! A blue-eyed goat! What is the world coming to?" But he sounded afraid and he gave Erland another good poke with his stick.

"Please don't hit me," Erland said. "I will do you no harm. I am a traveller on my way to the sea."

The man was even more frightened when Erland spoke. "You have no need to be afraid," said Erland. "I am a man just like you, but I am under a spell. If you will help me to the sea, the spell will be broken and I shall reward you with anything you ask."

"You will?" The man's eyes bulged with greed. "Would you give me a cow?"

"I would give you a cow."

The man's eyes narrowed. "All I have to do is sell you to a circus. You're worth more than any cow."

"I shall give you as much and more than any circus after I return from the sea," Erland replied.

"*After?*" said the man. "Give it to me now."

"I cannot pay you until I return. But now, please, help me to the sea."

"Not likely," the man said, giving him another poke. "It's a travelling circus for you. I've made up me mind."

Erland made a great show of sighing and said, "All right, then. I can see you're determined. And as I'm sure you're clever too, you'll know that we shall have to travel by night so that no one sees my eyes. Unless," and here Erland attempted a casual shrug, "unless you could make me heavy eyebrows."

"Eyebrows?" said the man.

"To hide my blue eyes. All you have to do is cut some hair from my body."

The man didn't relish travelling by night, and so, taking instructions from Erland, he made the eyebrows. With them Erland found it rather difficult to see, and he imagined he must look very hairy indeed, but he felt sure he would pass for a normal goat, just as long as he remembered not to speak!

The first part of his plan had gone well. But the second part—his escape—would not be so easy. The man had already tied a stout rope around Erland's neck and, as they set out for market, he held it in a very tight grip.

When Corille wakened in the morning and found Erland no longer in the garden, she ran at once to the palace.

"Oh, Galaad—your Highness," she cried. "The sea water. There wasn't enough. He's worse off now than he ever was. And this morning he's gone. I think he's on his way to the sea. I must follow him."

"You can't go alone," said Princess Meera.

"We must search for him together," said the Prince. "At once. The three of us."

"And," said the Princess's Fairy Godmother, who appeared before them, unexpectedly, glittering and shining, "you must fight magic with magic. There is no other way."

She handed them each a gift.

To Princess Meera, she gave the power of invisibility; to Prince Galaad, the strength of ten; while to Corille, she merely gave a pretty scarf which Corille wound tightly round her neck.

They took a horse apiece, food and water in their saddle bags, and their three magical gifts.

None of them knew exactly where the Wizard's Land began, but they rode through the beautiful countryside with hopes high, Corille searching eagerly for any sign of Erland. She couldn't be quite sure, but she thought the scarf made her eyesight better and her heart less troubled. And when, after some hours, the weather changed from pleasantly hot to freezing, she thought the scarf was even keeping her warm.

Then the snow began—softly at first. Soon the whole world was white with it. Corille and Princess Meera, who had never seen snow before, were delighted. But Prince Galaad was anxious, fearing the Wizard's tricks. Before long the wind increased and the snow stung them like a mass of needles which made it impossible for them to see. Prince Galaad, afraid that they might get separated from each other, took a rope from his saddle bag and tied the bridles of the three horses together. A white frost had formed around the horses' eyes and nostrils and small icicles hung from their chin-straps.

"We can't go on much longer," Prince Galaad said. "We need shelter for the night."

At that moment, Corille who was peering into the blizzard, cried, "A barn! What luck!"

It was a good solid building with a door that shut tightly, and horse-stalls and hay. Moreover, the magic scarf, stretched out to its full length, just covered the three of them exactly.

Snug and warm beneath the scarf, Princess Meera, Prince Galaad and Corille were soon fast asleep and dreaming.

"If I could only escape here," thought Erland when they arrived at the busy market place. But before going off in search of a circus, the man tied Erland firmly to a post. And although Erland pulled and strained at the rope and rubbed his body against the knot, he remained tied fast.

Then he noticed two boys standing nearby. One was fingering the blade of a knife. "I bet your knife isn't sharp enough to cut the goat's rope," Erland said. The boy, thinking it was his friend who spoke, gave the rope a mighty swipe with the blade and cut it clean through.

Erland was free.

What sights there were at the market! People were selling fruits and vegetables and freshly baked bread which made Erland's mouth water. But he dared no more than pause until he came to the place the goats were traded and sold. There, among other goats, he hoped to remain unnoticed until he had decided what to do next. He had never seen so many goats before—striped goats, spotted goats, black goats, white goats and—surely it couldn't be—but yes, it was—the Venerable William himself. Erland's heart overflowed at the sight of his friend.

"I've been following you, my boy," said the Venerable William. "Just keeping a fatherly eye on you from a distance."

Erland wanted to reply but he wasn't sure he could still speak Goat, and before he had time to think how to get his tongue around it, a little old woman was peering into his

face, her nose so close to his that he was afraid she would see his eyes. Then he felt fingers digging into his back and he heard her say, "Poor skinny creature, this one. I'll give you one anak for him—it's all he's worth."

Erland's rope was grabbed firmly by the little old woman but she looked kinder than the man who had taken him to market. She gave a yank to his rope and set off at a brisk pace, complaining as she went, "It's tired I am, and we've far to go."

When, at last, she came to a large tree growing by the side of the road, she stopped. "We'll just settle down in the shade here and have a nice rest." With that, she made a smooth place in the grass, arranged her skirts around her and spread out her belongings, without once slackening her grip on the rope.

"Now that the weight's off my feet," she said, pulling Erland closer, "let's have a good look at you, you poor skinny beast you." And she lifted his shaggy eyebrows and gazed straight into his eyes. "I saw your beautiful blue eyes at the market, that's why I bought you," the old woman said. "Oh, we'll make a pretty penny between us, you and me."

"I don't want to make a pretty penny," Erland said, and the woman's eyes grew round as she heard him speak. A goat with blue eyes and the voice of a young man!

"I'm under a spell, old woman, and I want to go to the sea. If you will help me I'll..."

The old woman gave a long cackle of a laugh. "The sea," she said. "Why, there's no such thing as the sea.

"Best you come along with me and forget all about the sea.

"But, first off, we'll have a bite to eat and a little short nap, like." She rummaged about in her bag and found some black bread, which she ate hungrily—only as an afterthought throwing the crusts to Erland, as if he were a dog.

"Now a little drink," she said, taking a swig from her wineskin, and a nice little nap as the evening cools."

With that she stretched herself out on the soft grass, took a firm grip on Erland's rope, placed her belongings beneath her head and straight away fell asleep.

Erland waited patiently until dusk turned to darkness, then, little by little, he moved away from the old woman, pulling smoothly and slowly on the rope that linked them.

He had only another few inches to go, when the old woman gave a great snort and rolled over. Erland froze. He didn't dare move a muscle. Then, persuaded by the sound of her deep rhythmical breathing that she was once again asleep, he gave another long, slow tug on the rope.

And he was free.

Tired and hungry as he was, joy filled his heart. The bright star overhead would guide him and the full moon would light his way. Surely his troubles were now behind him.

But little did Erland know that he was just about to step across the boundary that separated the Kingdom of Ure from the Wizard's Land.

Luckily for Erland the Wizard was too busy to notice that Erland had crossed onto his land.

The Wizard was making a Blasting Rod—a Blasting Rod which would extend his power over the entire world. It could only be made on this night, in the light of the first full moon of the year.

He had already found the wild hazel tree that the magical undertaking called for, and he had prepared the ritual knife.

After weeks of searching, he had finally discovered the Bloodstone.

All his equipment—including the White Robe and Hat—were ready on the bank of the stream where he would take his ceremonial bath.

He had nothing further to do but follow the book of spells to the letter. Opening it at the page he knew almost by heart, he read once again: "On the night of the first full moon of the year, write the following signs on the White Robe with the Pen of the Art."

The Wizard was quivering with excitement. He had made the Pen of the Art from the left-most wing feather of a swallow, as the book directed. And he had said "Arboy, Narboy," as the spell required. Now, with the greatest care, he copied the signs from the book onto the Robe.

The Wizard stripped to the skin, and lowered his body into the stream. He rose, shivering and dripping, and dressed himself in the White Robe and Hat. Only now could he prepare the Rod itself.

The moon shone down upon him clear and full and his knife blade flashed in its white light. As he sliced through the wood of the hazel tree and sealed the cut branch with the Bloodstone, the night about him remained silent, still, and bathed in the moonlight.

Then, holding the branch aloft, his voice hoarse with emotion, he recited the magic words he had learned by heart: "I command you, great Beleel! Endow this wand with the power of thunderbolts and the force of lightning!"

With a sizzling fork of fire the lightning answered, followed by peal upon peal of thunder so powerful that the very ground beneath him shook.

Erland was making good time. The ground was smooth under his four fast hooves and the full moon made the night almost as light as day. Once he was surprised by a great zigzag of lightning, followed by peal upon peal of thunder. There were no clouds overhead but not far off, there seemed to be snow in a huge dense swirl, unseasonal and strange, and for a dizzying moment he felt the earth quake.

Towards morning the land became rough. Badger holes and scattered rocks forced him to slow his pace. He was tired and hungry and short of sleep. Suddenly the ground beneath him seemed to give way and he felt a searing pain in a front leg. When he tried to get to his feet, the leg buckled and collapsed beneath him.

Erland lay on the boulder-strewn land unable to move. He had never felt as weak and thirsty in his life and the pain in his leg filled his whole body. He watched the moon set. He watched daylight break. And as the sun rose into mid-heaven, he lost all hope of ever seeing Corille again, all hope of ever reaching the sea.

And then he heard, very far off, what sounded like horses picking their way among stones, and what might have been a bridle jingling.

Whoever they were, they were coming towards him. Erland lay motionless. His heart, as if to help him, seemed to stop beating. Then in the silence, he thought they were moving away.

He allowed himself to breathe again.

Far off he heard a voice. Corille's voice. He wondered if his ears were playing him tricks.

"Corille!" he called but he was so weak and parched with thirst, that her name on his lips was little more than a whisper. With an enormous effort he lifted his head but the effort was so great he fainted.

The next thing Erland knew, Corille was holding a water bottle to his lips. "He's alive! Oh, Erland, I am here."

"Corille!" said Erland. "Oh, Corille!"

Corille bound his leg with her scarf, and Prince Galaad lifted Erland very gently and placed him across the withers of Corille's horse.

Now that they had found Erland they were doubly impatient to reach the sea, but it was impossible to gallop the horses over such rocky ground. And when, at last, the country underfoot improved, they were all so hungry that they stopped in a grove of tall trees—an especially beautiful grove—and lifted Erland onto the grass and unpacked and ate the delicious food from their saddle bags.

"But how did you find me?" Erland wanted to know. "You couldn't possibly have known where I would be."

"We didn't know," said Princess Meera. "Not for sure. But Corille found the way."

"It's the Fairy Godmother's scarf," Corille explained. "It helps me see."

The horses grazed contentedly nearby. Birds sang in the branches overhead. Without thinking Erland stood up on his four legs just as if he had forgotten that one of them wouldn't support him.

"Erland, you've walked!" cried Corille.

"So I have," said Erland, surprised. "So I have!"

Corille removed the scarf from his leg. "Does it hurt?" she asked. Erland shook his head. "Not the least bit."

"It's the scarf," said Corille. "I wonder what else it can do?" She wrapped it once again around her neck and tied it firmly.

"Look!" said the Princess Meera suddenly. "The trees. They're moving!"

And it was true. Their branches were now tightly entwined, woven together like a basket, and their trunks were advancing relentlessly towards each other.

"Quick," said Corille. "The horse!" and she grabbed the reins of Prince Galaad's horse and pulled it to safety, a split second before the two tall trees between which it had been grazing came together with a loud clang as if they were metal doors.

"We're trapped!" Erland said in dismay. What had once been separate trees were now joined together in a tight palisade.

"We must climb them," said Princess Meera, an excellent tree-climber herself. But as she spoke she realized that even though Erland had four good legs again, it would be impossible for him to climb. And they couldn't abandon their horses.

Prince Galaad was grave. "This can only be the work of the Wizard," he said.

"A warning. From now on we must be especially alert. We must remember our strengths. We must remember the new powers the Fairy Godmother gave us."

"We know Corille's scarf can heal, provide heat, and give the wearer better eyesight. You will have to be our eyes, Corille."

"And you must never forget," he said to Princess Meera, "that you can become invisible."

"But I don't know how. Do you think I just wish?"

"Try," they all said, and waited.

The Princess tried. Nothing happened. "Try harder," said Prince Galaad. Princess Meera scrunched up her eyes. "Harder still," said Prince Galaad. And she screwed up her face as tight as a fist.

And then, slowly, she began to fade. She grew paler and paler and paler until she had disappeared entirely and her voice came to them from empty space.

"Bravo!" they cried. "You've done it!"

"I have?" said Princess Meera. "So I have!" And then her voice wavered. "How do I come back?" she asked in alarm.

"Wish!" said Prince Galaad. "You have to wish as hard as you did before." And there she was, very pale at first, but gradually becoming darker and more visible.

Princess Meera was rather pleased with herself. With practise, she found she could come and go in a twinkling.

"Now let's see what my sword can do," said Prince Galaad. He slashed at the wall of trees, and it was as if his sword were an axe and he were ten men with ten axes, for he cut an opening wide enough for all of them and their horses to escape.

Beyond the tree circle, the country continued as before. For the moment there was no sign of the Wizard or his tricks.

Wildflowers grew in the grasses and gave off a sweet scent as they rode. Erland trotted happily beside them. A great white gull flew overhead and surprised them all. "It's a seabird," Prince Galaad shouted and they gave a loud cheer.

"I can smell the sea!" Corille exclaimed. Nobody else could. "It's the scarf," she said, tossing it to the Princess who shared it with Erland and Prince Galaad.

Now that they could all smell the sea, they were in high spirits and in a very great hurry to be on its shore.

Then Corille cried, "There it is!"

And there it was—almost within reach. A golden beach was all that separated them. And where it sparkled and danced in the sun, its blue was nearly blinding, and it was more beautiful than any of them remembered.

Erland, unable to wait another minute, was rushing across the sands to the salty water, as fast as his legs would carry him. Princess Meera, Corille and Prince Galaad, utterly forgetting the Wizard, were staring at the scene entranced, when—without warning and beyond possibility—the entire sky became black, and the blue sea changed to sullen pewter. Lightning flashed and thunder rolled and the horses whinnied and reared in terror.

"On your guard!" It was Prince Galaad's voice, commanding. They braced themselves for what was to come. And there, between them and the tempestuous sea, stood the Wizard. He wore a black cloak as shiny as coal, and a greenish glow around his body made him enormous in the half-light. His eyes burned like black fire, and in the darkness that surrounded him they imagined a thousand invisible evil forms.

"Trespassers!" hissed the Wizard. It was as if the lightning spoke. "You shall be punished for this."

He whirled the folds of his great black cloak around Princess Meera and caught her within its inky darkness.

But search the folds of his cloak as he would, the Princess wasn't there. She had totally disappeared. Baffled and angry, he lunged for Corille. But at that moment Prince Galaad attacked. Taken off guard, the Wizard stumbled, flung out his arm for balance and caught Corille with his sword. She swayed for a moment, then collapsed. Blood flowed from a wound on her shoulder.

In a frenzy of rage, the Wizard leaped forward with such force that had Prince Galaad not jumped nimbly aside he would have been felled.

But the Prince summoned all his strength and attacked. Back and forth they struggled, the Wizard and the Prince, as the storm raged about them. The Wizard was taller by a head than Galaad, and as thick through as a barrel. But Prince Galaad's lightness made him fast and sure-footed, his youth gave him endurance and the Godmother's gift gave him the strength of ten. When the Wizard began to tire, Prince Galaad, still not winded, pressed harder.

The Wizard regained his breath, and in a mighty voice that seemed to address the storm itself, he roared: "Oh, Great Beleel! My Blasting Rod!" And like a bolt of lightning, the magic weapon appeared in his hand, and with it he dealt Prince Galaad blow upon blow.

Galaad half fell. Quick to see his advantage, the Wizard moved in for his final stroke. But at that moment, within inches of his Blasting Rod, the Princess appeared and just as suddenly disappeared, an unexpected will-o-the-wisp, that astonished the Wizard and distracted him.

Those few seconds were all Prince Galaad needed to recover. He pressed forward, struck the Blasting Rod from the Wizard's grasp, and forced him backwards onto the beach.

Terror struck the Wizard as he felt the sand beneath his feet.

His eyes swivelled in his head. His arms flailed helplessly. "Beleel!" he roared above the storm, "Beleeeel," and his voice broke like an iron bar breaking.

"Now!" cried Prince Galaad, and together he and Princess Meera pushed and shoved the great, black, struggling body down the beach. Below the high tide line it crumpled suddenly as if it had no muscles or bones. And then it fell, a heap of coal on the sands. A dead weight, powerless, shapeless, black as night.

"To the sea," Galaad called to Princess Meera. "We must drag him to the sea."

"Not the sea!" sobbed the terrified Wizard. "No, no, not the sea!" But he was too weak to resist. And as Prince Galaad and Princess Meera rolled him into the shallows, the storm clouds suddenly vanished, the wild wind dropped and the sun came out and made the grey sea blue and the dark sands gold again.

When Erland had begun his joyful rush across the sands, the beautiful waters were calm and blue. But as he entered their shallows a powerful undertow knocked him off balance and sucked him out to sea. When he came up for air, mountainous waves broke over him, filled his eyes and his nostrils with water and tossed him about like driftwood. Struggling to stay alive, Erland had no time to notice that he was no longer a goat.

Then as suddenly as the storm had arisen, the winds dropped, and the sea became calm again. Erland shook the water from his head, and swam ashore. Standing in the shallows he looked at himself with wonder. Boots instead of hooves. Soggy clothes instead of goat hair. Forgetter had completely vanished. He was Erland—the same Erland who had run up onto the Wizard's land to pick a rose.

And here, in his hand, was the rose itself.

He scanned the shore for Corille but could see no sign of her. Calling, he ran across the sands and up the grassy slope where the horses grazed. There, to his surprise and delight, stood the Venerable William. Erland rushed to greet him. He had said no more than, "William!" when the words died on his lips. For the Venerable William was standing guard over Corille who lay motionless on the ground, her face as pale as ash.

"Oh, Corille!" Erland cried, forgetting William and dropping to his knees by her side. Blood flowed through the sword wound in her shoulder.

"Corille, I am here Corille. Do you see me?"

Corille opened her eyes, looked deep into Erland's and smiled.

Clumsily, then, with his newly regained hands, he unwound the scarf from her neck and gently bound her wound with it. So great were its healing powers that almost at once the blood was stanched. Colour slowly returned to her cheeks.

She was soon strong enough to sit up and look at him. "Erland!" she said with wonder, and she took his hand in hers and turned it over. "No more hooves," she said. "Stand up so I can see you."

"And here is the rose," said Erland, "the rose I picked for you all that long time ago."

And then they heard great cries from the beach, and they were reminded of the Wizard.

"Oh, look!" cried Erland. "Look!"

It was as if the sky and the sea were one—blue without break—so invisible was their join. The sand might have been made from precious stones, so brilliantly did it shine.

An extraordinary hush had fallen over the world. Sea birds hung suspended in the bright air. The horses stopped eating and lifted their heads from the grass—like horses entranced.

Then as Corille, Erland and the Venerable William watched, they saw the Princess Meera and Prince Galaad, dripping with sea water and laughing, walking towards them across the shining sands. And, almost impossible to believe, between the Prince and the Princess—his arms around their shoulders, and a good head taller than the Prince—was the most beautiful being they had ever seen.

His skin was of a silvery hue, his eyes and his hair were golden, and he gave off a great light that bathed them in its radiance.

"Dear Prince, dear Princess," he was saying as the three of them joined Corille and Erland and the Venerable William, "in return for the help you have given me, I give you this land—land which had for so long been known as 'the Wizard's Land.' It was under a black spell, just as I was myself. Now that I am no longer the Wizard and my land can no longer harm innocent travellers, I join it to the Kingdom of Ure, over which you will one day reign." As he spoke the light around him increased until they had to shade their eyes in order to see him.

"Return with us to Ure and live with us there," urged Prince Galaad.

And Princess Meera added, "Oh, do! Oh, Please! Our country is yours. Please come!"

Smiling, he shook his head. "My home is elsewhere. Now that I am free I must return to it. But we shall meet again. I promise."

And before their eyes, in the bright of day, he vanished.

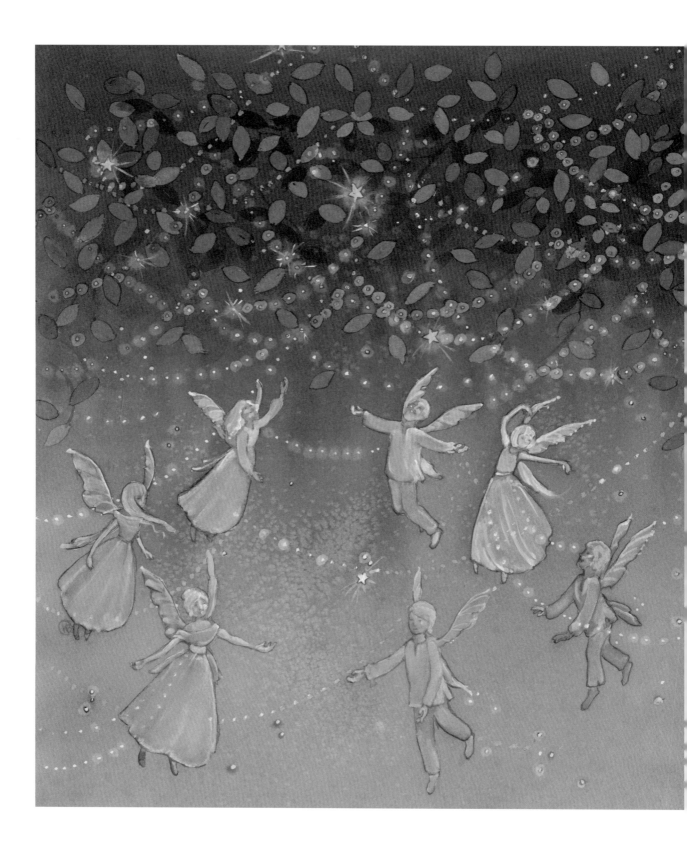

THE SKY TREE

The King and Queen were old. They had ruled their country wisely and well for many years. No one had ever gone hungry in Ure for the granaries were always full. Traders came from the four corners of the world to buy the crystallized fruits for which the country was famous. When royalty from other kingdoms wanted jewels for their crowns, or rings for their fingers, they sent messengers to Ure because its rubies were as red as pigeon`s blood and its sapphires as blue as the sea.

One day the Queen and King—Meera and Galaad to their friends—were strolling slowly through the palace grounds with Treece, their only son. The Queen (who walked with a slight limp) said, "I would so like to see the Wizard again." She inclined her head slightly towards the King to hear his reply. "So would I! So would I!" said the King.

"The Wizard?" Treece was suddenly interested. "What Wizard?"

"Have we never told you?" asked his mother vaguely.

"Tell me now," said Treece. "Please tell me now."

The Queen and the King exchanged glances, and then the Queen began. "A long time ago, before my father died and you were born, Ure was a landlocked kingdom. Travel was not as common then as it is today and the people of Ure had never seen the sea..."

"They didn't believe in it, either," the King laughed.

"Didn't believe in the sea!" Treece exclaimed.

"For some people, if they have never seen a thing, it's hard for them to believe in it. Unless it is love," he said dreamily. "Or rage, perhaps."

"...more importantly, the lands bordering the Eastern Sea belonged to a wicked Wizard," the Queen continued, picking up where she had been interrupted. "Your father knew him well."

"Too well," the King said. "He turned me into a goatherd."

"But I thought you were a goatherd—when you were a boy, I mean."

"Quite right, Treece," the King replied. "The first time I was a goatherd by birth and occupation. The second time, I was a goatherd by magic—black magic. The Wizard cast a spell upon me. Then, later still, after your mother and I were married, we met the Wizard again, face to face. And we fought."

"Fought!" said Treece. "But we don't fight in Ure."

"Your father was very brave," the Queen said, ignoring his remark.

"And your mother was very clever," added the King proudly. "It was a terrible fight. He used his Magic Blasting Rod."

"Did you kill him?" asked Treece.

"In a kind of a way," said his mother. "We forced him into the sea and…"

"Did he drown?" asked Treece. "No, he couldn't have drowned, for you want to see him again. Oh, do go on!"

"What we didn't know," continued the King, "was that the Wizard, too, was under a spell, and once in sea water he was no longer a wicked Wizard with a Blasting Rod, but a beautiful young man—as bright as the sun. The sea, you understand, can break such spells."

"Silvery and golden," said the Queen. "I should love to see him again. I think of him all the time."

"Where is he now?" Treece was practical as well as interested.

"That's just it," said the Queen and King together. "We don't know. You see, he said goodbye and then—he vanished. Into thin air."

"He couldn't just vanish!" said Treece. "It isn't possible."

"Many things are not possible." said the King, "and yet…" He shrugged. "It is not possible for a goatherd to marry a Princess. But it happened. It is not possible for a person to vanish into thin air. But the Wizard did. Before our eyes. Like that." The King snapped his fingers.

"Not before telling us that he would come back," the Queen said. "But he never has."

"Then you must search the kingdom for him," Treece said.

"Oh, he's not in Ure," his father replied. "Not anywhere here. You see, he went home."

"What do you think about Treece?" the King asked, when he and the Queen were alone together. "Do you think he can rule the Kingdom when we are gone?"

"I think he would make a fine ruler. He's a good boy. Honest and kind. Considerate, too."

"But is he strong?" asked the King. "And brave? Could he face uncertainty and danger?"

"If the occasion arose, I am sure he could. He has never had a chance to prove himself because we have had no wars during our reign." She looked at the King. "You don't foresee danger, do you?"

"No, no, no. Of course not. It is just that a good ruler must be able...," the King began, but he could see the Queen was not listening.

"I really would like to see the Wizard again," she said. "He did say he'd come back. Didn't he?"

"I'm not sure," said her husband. "I thought he said we would meet again."

"There you are!" The Queen was mildly triumphant. "How could we see him if he didn't come back?"

"We might go to him," said the King.

The Queen shook her head sadly. "But if we don't know where he is, where would we go?"

The King was silent. Thinking. "I have an idea," he said at last. "Let us talk to Erland and Corille and see what they remember."

Corille and Erland had also known the Wizard well—too well. He had cast a spell upon both of them that had turned them into goats! That was many years ago when the Queen was Princess Meera and the King was a young goatherd.

Corille and Erland had been with them later on that extraordinary day when they had forced the wicked Wizard into the sea. They had been there, too, when he had emerged dripping—silvery and golden—no longer a wicked Wizard but a being such as they had never before seen or imagined. A being they could never forget.

"He did say he would come back, didn't he?" Meera was certain Corille and Erland would agree.

But neither one of them could remember.

"Didn't he say something about going home?" Erland asked.

They were all quiet, trying to remember. He was so silvery and golden, so full of laughter and light. So tall. Different entirely from any of them. They longed to see him, each one of them. But they did not know how to begin to look.

"What about your Fairy Godmother?" Corille asked Meera, suddenly. "Wouldn't she help? She did once."

"My Fairy Godmother!" Meera exclaimed. "I had almost forgotten about her. She only ever came when I needed her very badly, and it's years since I've needed anything at all. Why, I don't know where she is or even how to find her."

"Why don't you just call her, the way you did before?" Corille suggested.

And so Queen Meera called. Out loud she called. She called every day for a week. Nothing happened. She called every day for a month. And still nothing happened.

"What do you think I should do now?" she asked Galaad.

"We must just go on believing she will come," he said.

One night when they were sitting on their balcony looking at the stars, the King—telescope to eye—said, "There's a most extraordinary object in the sky. Look!" and he handed the telescope to the Queen.

"A bar," said the Queen. "A pearly bar."

As they watched, it rushed towards them at a remarkable speed. Then, immediately overhead, it stopped, and began a slow descent until its lower end came to rest on the railing of their balcony—a great pearly bar reaching from the stars. It gave off an astonishing light.

And who should come down it, as if it were a flight of stairs, but the Fairy Godmother herself? She glittered like diamonds.

"You look as if you are made of fire," the Queen said, her face shining with pleasure.

"Fairies are made of fire," the Godmother answered.

"Fiery Godmother," said the King, laughing at his own joke, but at the same time understanding something he had not understood before.

"You needed me," the Fairy Godmother said, "so I came. How can I help you?"

"We would like to find the Wizard," the Queen said.

"Ah-h-h-h!" said the Fairy Godmother. "There are many who would like to find him."

"And we don't know where to look," said the King.

"Where have you looked?" the Fairy Godmother asked.

"Well, actually, nowhere—yet," said the King. "You see, he said he had to go home, and we don't know where home is."

"It is—everywhere," said the Fairy Godmother, and she waved her wand in a great circle which took in all of heaven and earth. "You must search," she said. "Land, sea and air."

"We are old," said the Queen. "Searching is no longer as easy as when we were young."

"But finding is sometimes easier." The Fairy Godmother placed her small shining foot on the bottom of the pearly bar which, like an escalator, took her up, up and out of sight before they could open their mouths to say goodbye.

"Finding is sometimes easier," said the King and the Queen over and over again in the weeks that followed. Not that it was proving so for them.

To begin with, because they themselves could no longer travel, they had to call upon the realm's Searchers—men and women with eyes as sharp as hawks' and noses and ears as keen as dogs'. The Searchers were specially trained to find missing objects, missing pets and missing persons. They were not police. Ure had no need for police, but it did need Searchers. They found many things, some that were deeply hidden, like memories and dreams, to say nothing of rings dropped down wells, cats stuck in trees, and people who had taken the wrong road home in the dark.

The King and Queen knew that if the Wizard were anywhere in the kingdom, or even in the neighbouring lands, the Searchers would find him.

The first report of a sighting was in the capital of Ure itself. The Searchers had not actually seen the Wizard, but someone answering to that description had been seen—and not long ago. And not far from the palace grounds, either. No one could say exactly when, or exactly where. But a tall man had been sighted, very tall—and all silvery and golden.

After that, not a day went by but a new account of the Wizard reached them from somewhere. He had been seen in the high mountain passes. Or helping the workers pick fruit in the orchards. Once he had been seen walking on the waves. And everyone who had seen him claimed to have felt better afterwards. But none could say where he was now, where he had come from, or why he stayed for so short a time among them. Nor did they know why, sometimes, he walked away, while sometimes he just vanished, leaving the people shaking their heads with wonder.

Each day the Searchers sent their reports to the Palace. And now everyone in the Kingdom was on the alert for the Wizard, whom they knew to be there among them, moving like summer lightning—bright, beautiful, but always beyond reach.

It was clear to the King and Queen that the Searchers had seen him over and over again. But like a fish that no net could hold, he was found only to be lost again—not from memory, of course, but from there, wherever it was he had been seen.

So the King and Queen recalled the Searchers to the Palace and thanked them and sent them back to searching once again for all the objects, pets and people that had disappeared during the time they had been looking for the Wizard.

"Did you find the Wizard?" asked the Fairy Godmother, awash with starlight as she came once again at the Queen's call.

"Yes and no," said the Queen. And she told the Fairy Godmother the whole story, which of course, she already knew.

"You have searched the land and the sea," said the Godmother. "The only place left is the air."

The King, the Queen, and the Fairy Godmother were together on the balcony. How brilliantly the night stars shone! The constellation Schooner was like a great ship of lights above them. The King and the Queen were craning their necks in wonder when, in an unexpected rush of air, they found themselves on board that pearly bar and rising high into the sky. Incomparably high.

Below, their palace with its courtyards and banquet rooms seemed nothing more than a cluster of bright dots, while the earth itself, pricked with the lights of Ure and Ure's neighbouring kingdoms, might have been the night sky as they had seen it many times from their balcony.

How wonderful this ascent into the night, with shooting stars glowing, and disappearing all around them. And was it their eyesight or the effect of the starlight that made them young again? When the Queen looked at the King he seemed hardly more than a boy. And when the King looked at the Queen, he saw the black-haired Princess he had fallen in love with when he was a goatherd.

Then the pearly bar slowed and came to a stop, and they found themselves in a world of rainbows. Free of the air of earth, colors were different. To their surprise, the Fairy Godmother was purest violet. Beside her was another being, as beautiful as she, who was deepest indigo; and next to her a blue, then a green and a yellow and an orange and a red. And beyond them were ranks and ranks of other beings—some multi-coloured, and some almost transparent like crystal—who made way for a stream of perfect smaller beings, as bright as fireflies, who accompanied the Queen of Faerie. She was surely the most beautiful person in all the heavens, or wherever they were in this realm of air. Great crowds assembled around her in rainbow formation when she sat on a cushion of cloud and beckoned the King and Queen to sit beside her.

She offered them food unknown on earth, and delicious drinks out of goblets of crystal that reflected all the colors of the rainbow and, as they ate, fairies sang songs sweeter than anything heard in Ure, in keys that only Faerie knew. And when the dancing began, the King and the Queen found that their feet danced as fast as fairies' feet.

"Guests at my court," said the Queen of Faerie, when the dancing ended, "always receive a gift. I grant their heart's desire."

The King and Queen spoke as one. "Our heart's desire is to find the Wizard."

"One heart's desire for two people!" said the Queen of Faerie. "Remarkable. In that case you may have a lesser wish, as well."

The King and Queen hadn't thought of lesser wishes, so strong was their desire to see the Wizard.

"What about Corille and Erland?" Galaad suggested, and Meera agreed.

In a flash Corille and Erland appeared, rubbing their eyes as if they had just wakened, looking about them in wonder. And they, too, were young, just as they had been when they first met Meera and Galaad.

The Queen of Faerie offered refreshments, and told them that if they could name it, she would give them each their heart's desire.

"My heart's desire?" said Corille. "Oh-h-h . . . happiness. Eternal happiness," and she held out her hand to Erland.

And Erland, in his turn, seeing Corille as beautiful as she had ever been, said his heart's desire was that he and Corille should remain together until the end of time.

Overhead, an enormous chandelier filled the night sky—or so it appeared. It was made of stars and stars and more stars. And yet it was a tree. Astonished by its height, Meera and Galaad and Corille and Erland surveyed it. It was as if they were lying on their backs in Ure and looking up into the branches of the tallest tree in the land, one that was covered with thousands of lights.

"The Sky Tree," said the Queen of Faerie, and a shiver went through them at the name. "It leads to the Wizard."

Its many branches and glittering lights were bewildering, and as they stared into what must surely have been infinity, they felt like mere dots in all that space.

"The Sky Tree leads to the Wizard?" Meera asked, in a small voice, "It looks awfully difficult."

"Oh, it is difficult," said the Queen or Faerie. "But it's not impossible."

"What should we take with us?" asked Corille, troubled by the thought of the climb.

"That you will have to decide for yourselves," said the Queen of Faerie. "I can't even advise you, for you are leaving my realm and going to one about which I know little."

"I shan't take anything," said Meera. "Only the clothes I have on."

"We'll need our hands free for climbing," Galaad said. And as they removed their crowns and jewels they saw that, in this realm of Faerie, the most precious stones from Ure looked like nothing more than coloured glass, and Ure's gold was without luster.

"You can leave your jewels, if you like," said Corille, "but I'm going to take my necklace and my ring. They're light. And they're pretty. And I love them."

They said goodbye to the Queen of Faerie, and the beautiful creatures of her court assembled to see them leave, for it was not often that anyone dared climb the Sky Tree.

"You are going where I am no longer of any help," Meera's Fairy Godmother said, and shed a tear. "I shall not even be able to hear you if you call."

Galaad looked at Meera. "You first," he said, remembering how well she had climbed trees when she was young. "I'll be right behind you."

Meera jumped, grabbed the lowest branch of the Sky Tree, and swung herself up.

The climbing was easy at first, for they were young and nimble and strong. Corille and Erland were especially happy, remembering the last time all four of them had been together on the adventure which had ended with their meeting the Wizard face to face. And now here they were on a greater adventure still, climbing the Sky Tree which would lead them to the Wizard once again.

Seen from the Land of Faerie, the stars that formed the tree had appeared very close together, but now those same stars were separated by great airy spaces through which the climbers had to swing like trapeze artists. "Don't look down," said Corille, who just had, and whose head was spinning. "Could we stop? I'm starving. Did anyone bring food?"

"I've found a perfect place to rest," said Meera from above. And she had. It was kind of a nest made from small soft stars which glowed and gave off a comfortable warmth.

Nearby, bright fruits grew on silver vines. Corille picked one and held it in her hand. It gave off a faint light and fragrance. They all looked at it a long time. They wondered if it was poison. Then Corille, who was the hungriest, took a tiny bite. "Mmm-mm!" she said. "Delicious! Have some." The smallest bite made them feel as though they had eaten an entire meal.

Refreshed, they began to climb again. The Sky Tree was just like any ordinary tree except for its size and the fact that its branches shone, and its leaves, when touched, fell in a shower of sparks only to grow again in a burst of light.

At first there had been no birds in the branches, but suddenly the leaves were full of them—birds of all kinds—invisible in the darkness but whistling and singing and talking. One splendid parrot kept repeating, "Right this way. Right this way," as he led them from the night through which they had been climbing into a land, sunny and beautiful, with rushing streams and natural fountains.

"How beautiful!" Corille cried, happy at the sight of green fields again. "And look—people! Laughing and dancing!"

In no time at all Meera, Galaad, Corille and Erland were dancing too. Such steps they danced, such intricate, fast steps.

"It's wonderful!" said Meera as she and Galaad ran dripping from the stream. But suddenly, she was reminded of how she and Galaad had run dripping from the sea with the Wizard between them, and that memory, although sweet, was like a pain in her heart. "Galaad, we must go," she said. "We must find the Wizard."

"Perhaps he's here," said Corille who did not want to leave.

Meera shook her head. "He's not here. I feel sure of it." And Galaad agreed.

So they began once again on their climb to find the Wizard.

Because they had grown accustomed to daylight, the night world beautiful as it was, felt strange to them.

Everything was more difficult now. They were clumsy and slow. Even Meera had trouble finding a handhold, and Galaad had barely the strength to pull himself up.

Then from the darkness below Corille called, "Help! Oh, help! I—I'm stuck."

Erland, first to reach her, found her necklace was entangled in a thicket of glittering twigs. "It won't take a minute," he said, for it looked simple. But it was not.

"I can't move," Corille said.

Galaad joined them. It was as if the twigs were alive. No matter what they did to untangle the necklace, the twigs tangled it again. "You'll have to take it off," Galaad said, finally. "We'll disentangle it when you're free." Corille undid the clasp, and Erland tried again. But nothing they did to work it loose had any effect. It just got more and more tangled. Finally Corille, sad because she loved her necklace, decided she must leave it behind.

Great birds moved in the branches overhead—dark birds. Their feathers shone like jet. The stars of the Sky Tree dimmed and went out. One by one.

"This way, this way," croaked the birds, and they cackled with terrible laughter as they led the climbers into a darkness so black that they could no longer see each other.

"I'm frightened here," said Corille. "I want to go back to that beautiful place where everyone was happy."

Erland, whose only wish was to be with Corille, wherever she was, agreed.

But Meera and Galaad said they must find the Wizard.

"Oh do come with us," Corille pleaded. "It was lovely there and we've all been friends for so long and I know we'd be happy."

But Meera and Galaad had to go on.

And so the couples parted. And as Corille and Erland began their descent, Meera and Galaad struggled upwards again through what was now a pitch-black night, with only the taunting cackles of the black birds as their guides. "I must say I'm a bit frightened myself," said Meera.

"We'll be all right," Galaad replied. "We've got each other. And whether we like them or not, we've got the birds."

"This way. This way," the feathered creatures croaked. "This way."

Meera began to tire. "Galaad, we must stop. I can't go any further. I can't see to climb. I'm hungry and thirsty and tired."

But the only answer was the terrible cackle of the black birds' laughter, followed by silence. The most enormous total silence.

"Galaad!" Meera called, suddenly terrified. "Galaad, where are you? Oh, Galaad!" How could he have left her without any warning or word of goodbye? If he had fallen, surely he would have cried out and she would have heard him. But if he were anywhere near he would have answered.

"I'm all alone," Meera said to herself, unbelieving. She crouched on a narrow branch—neither comfortable nor safe. For support, she hung on to a smaller branch above her head. If she lost her balance for even a second she would fall through that endless all-surrounding night—the night in which she had lost Galaad. She could see nothing. Hear nothing. "Oh, Galaad," she cried, "where can you be? How could we have become separated like this?"

Fingers touched her hand. For a moment she thought Galaad had returned. But almost immediately she knew that it was not Galaad. Whoever it was, was uncurling her fingers one by one. Loosening her grip on the branch. "No!" she called out in panic. "No! Go away! Please!" But as quickly as she gripped the branch afresh, those hidden fingers began again, uncurling her fingers one by one. And they were strong—stronger than she was.

Galaad didn't know what had happened. One moment he had been climbing in the dark with Meera, following the voices that called, "This way, this way," and the next he was all alone in a pitch-dark night, unable to see or hear anything at all. Worst of all he had lost Meera.

"Meera," he called. "Meera!"

Not even an echo answered.

The thought that she might have slipped and fallen filled his heart with dread. He called her again, "Meeeeera!"

At that moment something soft was placed over his mouth. How could he reach Meera if he could no longer call to find out where she was? And if he could not find her…. The thought was unbearable. He felt himself wrapped round and round with ropes, legs bound together, arms tied to his sides. If Meera should call him now, he would be unable to answer or move. He waited for something more to happen. Perhaps they would take him away, whoever they were. But having wrapped him up like a mummy, they seemed to have disappeared and left him alone in the dark and terrible silence.

He had no idea how long he had hung there gagged and helpless before he heard, quite clearly, the words the Wizard had spoken by the sea, all those years ago. "We shall meet again." The voice was nearby, almost inside him.

He concentrated with all his power on the memory of that silver and golden figure, and listened intently to hear what else he might say. And as he visualized the Wizard, a sprinkling of notes sounded in the silent night. At the same time the darkness filled with millions of grains of light, so tiny and so many—golden kernels pouring from a cornucopia—that they created a great luminous field.

Within it, like a body on fire, in a suit of lights, stood the Wizard.

A Wizard, of course, has the power to find any person who searches for him. It is almost as if that person is made of iron filings which the Wizard's magnet can attract.

And because Galaad had looked so hard for the Wizard, the Wizard found Galaad. In all that darkness, in all that silence, the Wizard found Galaad.

Meanwhile back in Ure, the King and the Queen were missing.

Treece was alarmed and puzzled. They had never disappeared before and, on those rare occasions when they had to go away, they had always told him ahead of time, and formally handed over their responsibilities in the presence of the Lord Chamberlain. This time they had just vanished.

When the attendant in the Royal Bedchamber said they had not slept in their bed; when the footmen in the dining hall said they had not arrived for their meals; when the Royal gardeners insisted they had not taken their daily walk in the gardens; and when the Master of the Horse swore that, no, he had not taken out the carriages nor driven their Majesties anywhere, nor had he saddled the Royal horses—then Treece called the Searchers once again. And he asked them to scour the kingdom for their King and Queen.

But the Searchers could find no one in the entire realm who had seen them. Surely, protested their subjects, their Majesties must be in the capital, ruling Ure as always. Surely they were somewhere in the palace, attending to the affairs of state.

But they were not.

That night Treece tossed and turned in his silken bed. Where could his parents have gone, saying nothing and disappearing utterly? He knew they had been looking for the Wizard. Had they, perhaps, walked off together to see if they could succeed where the Searchers had failed? But how could they have gone on foot, with his mother lame? And without anyone's seeing them? It was impossible.

Later that night, with none of his problems solved, Treece fell into a troubled sleep. He dreamed that his mother was calling him. Not just saying "Treece," lovingly, the way she had so many times in his life, but sounding so desperate, so filled with fear, that his heart turned over and he awoke.

Moonlight silvered his room. He was wide awake. Yet even awake he could still hear her voice calling and desperate. He longed to help her.

"Mother," he called back. "Mother, where are you?"

Then, thinking that his parents had perhaps returned, he ran to the Royal bedchamber and threw open the door, half expecting to see them in their bed where they should have been. But he was greeted by an eerie emptiness, made all the more empty by the silver moon shining in through one of the tall windows and casting a path of light across the room.

He could still hear his mother's voice, from somewhere, calling, "Treece. Treece."

"Tell me where you are and I will come to you," Treece cried.

And then it was as if the path of moonlight had gathered him up, for there he was on a pearly bar, rising through the night sky in a rush of air.

At first he thought he must be dreaming, for it had happened so suddenly, and nothing in his whole life has prepared him for such an experience. He felt as if he were floating, no longer a prisoner of gravity, and then he realized that he was not floating at all but sitting on something quite firm.

"I am your mother's Fairy Godmother," a voice said. "Can I help you?" Beside him stood a being more beautiful than anything he could have imagined.

"Oh, yes!" said Treece. "At least, I hope you can. My mother is calling me and I don't know where she is or how to find her."

"I cannot tell you where she is, but I can show you were she went."

The Fairy Godmother led him to the base of a giant tree. "Look up!" she said.

Unbelieving, he saw a tree, taller than any earthly tree. It seemed to be made of stars and it disappeared into the blackness of the night.

"You will have to climb it," the Fairy Godmother said. "That is what your mother did."

Treece once again wondered if he was dreaming. How could his mother have climbed any tree, let alone this one, when it was difficult for her to even walk. "Up there?" he asked. "But how—"

"She climbed," said the Fairy Godmother. "And you will have to follow."

Treece's heart sank. He had no head for heights. As a boy at school he had been ashamed when his friends had run along the railing of the bridge that crossed the river. Every time he had tried to do so his knees had turned to water and his head had spun. Since he had become a young man and, happily, he was no longer expected to run along railings, he had put it all out of his mind. But now, his mother needed him and the only way he could reach her was to climb into that vast and terrible space.

Gazing upward, wondering how to begin, he heard his mother's voice again. This time it was high above him, and it was calling, "Treece! Oh, Treece!"

"Mother, I am here. I am coming."

Shutting his eyes so that he was unable to see what so terrified him, he jumped for the lowest branch of that shining tree, and swung himself onto it. He knew that if he looked up into its branches, he would be dazzled by its maze of bewildering lights. And that if he looked down... but he did not dare look down. So he concentrated intently on climbing from branch to glittering branch.

After what seemed a very long time, he heard his mother's voice again. It was closer now, but weak. And he realized that she was not calling his name as he had thought. She was saying, "No. No. No. Oh, please. Please!"

"Mother!" he called, "it's Treece! I am coming..." But as he spoke the lights of the tree went out one by one and in the inky blackness he felt the dizzying emptiness below him and he had to force himself to keep going—gripping the branches firmly and feeling for good footholds as he went. Fingers now clutched at his clothes, pulled his hair, held him back. From his insecure position in the tree he tried to protect himself. But the fingers he couldn't see tweaked and pinched and were stronger than he was.

"Please!" His mother's voice was hardly more than a whisper.

Treece had no weapon to help him and he was not sure it would have done much good, anyway. He struggled on in the direction of his mother's voice, feeling as if he were trying to swim upstream in a river of air that was full of shoals and snags, and black—blacker than anywhere he had ever been in his life.

After what seemed a long time the Queen's voice sounded again. And this time it was closer still.

"I am coming," he managed to call. But as he opened his mouth, soft strong fingers filled it. Until now Treece had been uncertain how to fight this unseen enemy, but suddenly he knew it was not enough to protect himself. He must attack. And as he beat and kicked and bit his enemies with all the force left in him, a terrible scream filled the air.

His first thought was that it was his mother's last cry. But when, almost immediately, dozens of hands were plucking, pinching, and holding him—their fingers poking in his ears and eyes—he realized it had been his attacker's scream for help.

Nothing in his life had prepared Treece for what was happening. He had not fought in a war, for there had been no wars to fight; and in the wrestling sports—the nearest he had come to combat as a boy—he had never had to overcome an invisible opponent, or more than one opponent at a time.

Treece's mind was suddenly clear. He knew he had to free his arms and legs for fighting. From his precarious position on a branch he worked his way into a crotch of the tree, leaned against its broad trunk, and fought the only way he could—by biting, scratching, kicking, punching the merciless fingers he could not see. On and on he fought. On and on, until at last he had no strength left. Blackness engulfed him.

He did not know how long it was before he saw a tiny point of light which grew larger and larger, and in its blaze two figures that looked like his mother and father—but young, as young as he was himself. He blinked. It made no sense. His parents were old. His mother walked with a limp and was a little deaf and his father's beard was grey and his face was deeply lined. Yet here they were before his eyes and his mother was beautiful and her hair was black, and his father was like a young athlete with muscular brown arms and legs. And they were no longer wearing their crowns or robes of office. They were clothed in light.

Then Treece realized a remarkable thing. He understood in a flash that everyone in the world was the same age—no one younger or older than anyone else. He could not understand it, but he knew it to be true. Was there something in the air of the world that made people appear to be old or middle-aged or young? And not only people, he thought, but every living thing, animals and even fruits.

He had been so surprised by this curious thought and the sight of his youthful parents that he had not noticed the light in which they were flooded was coming from a third figure who glowed from within as if he were a sun.

Treece shaded his eyes to gaze at this astonishing golden being. An overwhelming love filled his heart. He knew he was looking at the Wizard. At the same time Treece felt himself pulled towards the Wizard as if by a powerful magnet, and as he joined the three of them in that great, bright space he was aware that the Wizard and his parents were parts of a whole. And he saw his parents gaze at the Wizard with a wonder and love such as he had never seen. And the same expression was on their faces when they turned to each other.

Treece felt a pang of disappointment as he realized the three of them belonged together while he, for some reason he could not understand, was an outsider. Then the Queen looked at Treece as a mother looks at her baby—unbelieving and protective and loving. And in that instant Treece knew that he belonged here, too, that this was his home, just as it was theirs, but that the time had not yet come for him to join them. There was still something he had to do.

"You are now King of Ure, my son," his father said, turning his youthful face towards him. "You must return at once, for the court is already preparing for your coronation." He laughed such a merry laugh that Treece found himself laughing too, even though he barely knew if he were happy or sad.

The King and Queen embraced their son, and Treece understood that before they could meet again he must return to Ure by himself and rule wisely and well as his parents had before him.

Then the Wizard, looking into Treece's eyes, spoke directly to him for the first time. And he repeated the promise he had made to Treece's parents many years ago.

"We shall meet again," he said.

A NOTE FROM THE AUTHOR

All my life I have loved fairy tales. When young, I was lucky enough to have parents who read them to me—parents who loved them too. Now that I am older, I approach them less literally and respond to them more deeply. They are tales of hope. They show me unexpected things about myself and the world. They are rich in reminders of perseverance and kindliness. And, even more important, they persuade me that another, invisible world can manifest itself within our three-dimensional, daily one.

In the light of all this, it is not surprising that I should want to write a fairy story myself—a traditional fairy story. But I was never able to do so. And then, one night, the phrase "blue blood" came into my head. *Webster* defines it—and I quote—as "membership in a noble or socially prominent family". *The Shorter Oxford*—to quote again—says, "tr. Sp. *sangre azul* claimed by certain families of Castile as being uncontaminated [sic] by Moorish, Jewish or other admixture; probably founded on the blueness of the veins of people of fair complexion."

"Blue blood"—sea-blue blood—so my idle thoughts ran. But, of course! Why hadn't I seen it before? "Blue blood" had nothing to do with class or race. It was a term applied to the wise, to those who, symbolically, had been to the sea—that mythical source of all life, the "great mother", which, in most cultures, represents wisdom, wholeness, truth—and as a result, in whose veins flowed, symbolically again, blood that was [sea] blue.

And as far as Royalty being "blue-blooded"—[royal blue, note!]—perhaps, in some Golden Age, "blue blood" had nothing to do with lineage and everything to do with wisdom; and that seeking his successor, the old King in the fairy tales was trying to find a young man as wise or, in my terminology, as "blue-blooded" as he. I can't think of a single tale in which the Kingdom automatically goes to the rightful heir.

But I am no scholar. I am no etymologist either, and I am not trying to persuade you of the rightness of my notion. Perhaps there was no Golden Age when Kings were chosen for their wisdom—perhaps that happens only in fairy tales. But, interestingly, on checking four historically wise rulers, I found that three—Solomon, Alexander the Great, and Charlemagne—had no clear titles to the kingdoms they ruled, and that the fourth—Haroun el-Rashid, Charlemagne's friend—had a curiously unconventional line of ascent.

So that is where my ruminations about "blue blood" led me; and how I came to write a traditional fairy tale in which a young man, in order to win the hand of the Princess, made the long journey to the sea. In so doing, he proved himself a wise and worthy successor to the old King.

P. K. Page is also an artist who paints under the name P. K. Irwin. She is the author of more than a dozen books of poetry, travel, short stories, and children's books. She has won numerous prizes, including the Governor General's Prize for Poetry, has eight honorary degrees, is a Companion of the Order of Canada, a member of the Order of British Columbia and a Fellow of the Royal Society of Canada.

Kristi Bridgeman lives in Saanich, B.C. with her husband and two children. She has illustrated several books. Her fine art pieces can be found at the Art Gallery of Greater Victoria and Sooke Harbour House Gallery.